Martin Bax,

lives of so many

the world

rience justice, fairness, freedom

nt values are our human rights.

Amnesty International protects people whose human rights have

been taken away, and helps us all to understand our human

rights better. Amnesty International has

two million members worldwide.

www.amnesty.org.uk

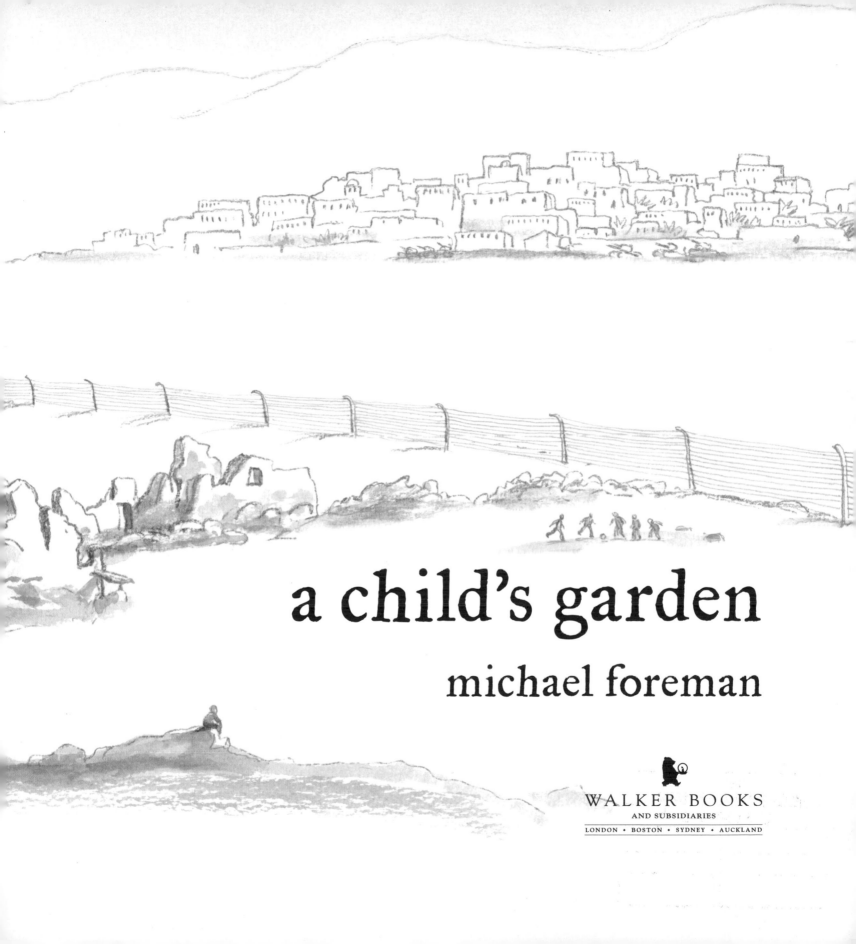

a child's garden

michael foreman

WALKER BOOKS

AND SUBSIDIARIES

LONDON · BOSTON · SYDNEY · AUCKLAND

The boy saw it after a night of rain,

a speck of green in the rubble, peeping up towards the sunlight. He moved some broken bricks so that nothing would fall and crush the tiny plant. He didn't know what sort of plant it was, a flower or a weed; he just knew it would struggle to survive.

The boy searched around and found an old can which held a little rainwater. He brought it to the plant.

"Drink up," he whispered. "Drink up."

The sun was climbing in the sky and the boy gave the plant shade with some old sacking and wire.

The boy's world was a place of ruin and rubble, ringed
by a fence of barbed wire. In the hot, dry summer the air was
thick with dust. Faraway hills shimmered in the haze. The
boy knew that cool streams flowed in those hills. He used
to go there with his father, but now the hills
were the wrong side of the wire.

Over the following weeks he cared for his secret garden. Soon the green tendrils reached to the high barbed wire fence. Now the boy could tell it was a vine – a grapevine.

It spread along the fence, and gave shade to its own tender roots which, in turn, sent out more shoots.

Birds and butterflies came bringing seeds and pollen on their wings. The garden grew. It was no longer a secret.

Friends came to sit in its shade
and it became a playground for the children.

Then, one day, soldiers came
and destroyed everything.
They threw the vine in
a ditch on the other
side of the wire.

The boy thought his heart would break.

Winter came.

The boy and his family shivered in the cold and damp of their ruined home.

Spring came late. After the first night of rain for weeks, the boy noticed green shoots all along the ditch. Some seeds from his vine must have survived the winter. He worried about the new shoots. He couldn't get close enough to water them. They were on the other side of the wire.

Then, one evening, he saw a little girl playing by the ditch.

She had a bucket and she was sprinkling water on the tiny plants.

Each evening she returned.
The boy hoped the soldiers wouldn't notice. But they
didn't seem to mind plants growing on their side of the fence.

Then, one day, the boy saw tiny specks of green peeping from the rubble where his garden had been.

"Look!" he yelled. "Come and see! My vine has come back!"

He began collecting water and once more tended his garden.
Soon it reached the wire where it became entwined with
the green tendrils from the little girl's side.

The barbed wire disappeared under leafy shade and the new garden became home once more to birds and butterflies.

Let the soldiers return, thought the boy.

Roots are deep and seeds spread.

One day the fence will disappear forever
and we will be able to walk again into the hills.

Other books by Michael Foreman

"Foreman's finest work to date."
The Sunday Times

ISBN: 978-1-4063-0533-3

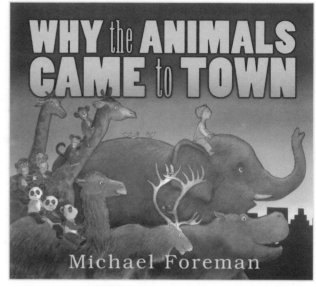

ISBN: 978-1-4063-1801-2

ISBN: 978-1-4063-1359-8

ISBN: 978-1-84428-495-5

First published 2009 by Walker Books Ltd, 87 Vauxhall Walk, London SE11 5HJ • This edition published 2010 • 10 9 8 7 6 5 4 3 2 1
© 2009 Michael Foreman • The right of Michael Foreman to be identified as author/illustrator of this work has been asserted by him in accordance with the Copyright, Designs and Patents Act 1988 • This book has been typeset in Fell Type • Printed in China • All rights reserved. No part of this book may be reproduced, transmitted or stored in an information retrieval system in any form or by any means, graphic, electronic or mechanical, including photocopying, taping and recording, without prior written permission from the publisher. • British Library Cataloguing in Publication Data: a catalogue record for this book is available from the British Library • ISBN 978-1-4063-2588-1

www.walker.co.uk